A Christmas Orphan

By James Howard Kunstler

ALSO BY JAMES HOWARD KUNSTLER

Fiction

The Jeff Greenaway Series
The Law of the Jungle
The Fall of the Ancients

The World Made By Hand Series
The Harrows of Spring
A History of the Future
The Witch of Hebron
World Made By Hand

A Safe and Happy Place
Big Slide
Maggie Darling, a Modern Romance
Thunder Island
The Halloween Ball
The Hunt
Blood Solstice
An Embarrassment of Riches
The Life of Byron Jaynes
A Clown in the Moonlight
The Wampanaki Tales.

Nonfiction

Too Much Magic
The Long Emergency
The City in Mind
Home From Nowhere
The Geography of Nowhere

A Christmas Orphan

A Novella

By James Howard Kunstler

The Greenaway Series
Book 1

Highbrow Press

Published in the United States of America

ISBN 978-0-9846252-6-0

Highbrow Press
PO Box 193
Saratoga Springs
New York, 12866

A Christmas Orphan

✳

IT IS A MOMENTOUS OCCASION when any child hears that he may not be the person he thinks he is, that he may even be an orphan, which, except for never being born, is the closest thing there is to being no person at all. Perhaps Jeff Greenaway, eleven years old, heard it wrong. This is quite possible since it was a thing *overheard* rather than told to him directly. He overheard it in the course of an argument between his parents. Being civilized city people from good backgrounds, his parents hardly ever quarreled.

But it was Christmas time, and Jeff's father had come home from the Friday night office party rather late (ten o'clock) and tipsy (he was *not* drunk) and bearing a reddish-pink smudge on his shirt collar (just a holiday peck from Gloria Oldfield, the boss's secretary, who was "almost sixty years old, for Godsake"), and altogether Jeff's mother was not amused.

Who knows what had gotten into her that day? There was a morning session with Dr. Krajak, the dentist, but just a cleaning and some investigative poking with the ghastly instruments, no drilling or, God forbid, root canal. There were the crowds at Bloomingdale's in the afternoon, a mob of women very much like herself, moiling through clouds of perfume samples—but to suggest it is a hardship to spend money at holiday time in New York City would strain anyone's credulity. Perhaps it was her time of the month—though there are things in this world of mystery that not even an omniscient narrator can tell. At any rate, after Jeff's father came home late that evening, he and Jeff's mother had a fight.

As it happened, Jeff was in his room enjoying an episode of *The Twilight Zone* on television. The show was about an elderly commuter who leaves the modern city on the 6:10 train and instead of getting home to the suburbs ends up in the turn-of-the-century small town of his youth—the *catch,* of course, being that he has died of a heart attack on the train and gone to heaven. Jeff never got to that part, however. He began to hear raised voices emanating from his parents' bedroom about the time that the old geezer in the TV show first stepped off the train into the quaint town of Drakesburg with its horses and buggies, its bandshell in the park, its shopkeepers with gartered shirtsleeves, and its kids happily rolling their hoops across the town square. Jeff's mother shouted clearly through the wall, "I never should have married you!"

This caught Jeff's attention. He reached for the TV's volume knob while his father replied—something too low to be understood—but then his mother shouted back, "Well, I wouldn't have either, except for the baby!"

An icy chill ran through Jeff's spinal fluxes as he intuitively grasped that the baby in question must have been himself, since he had no brothers or sisters. Again, Jeff's father made some reply, but his baritone voice was not as shrill as Jeff's mother's, and didn't carry well through the wall. To whatever he had said, Jeff's mother loudly retorted, "I suppose he wasn't your child!" That there might be any question about it was a notion that rocked the foundations of Jeff's selfhood. He was so shaken, in fact, that he did not recognize the sarcasm in his mother's voice when next she said, "That's right, I found him on the doorstep one fine morning, a little orphan in a willow basket!"

Jeff shrank away from the wall, papered with posters from his favorite horror movies, as though the various vampires, blood beasts, werewolves, and slavering anthropophagi had come alive. A burst of sobs—his mother's—was all that followed from beyond the wall. For a time, Jeff stared at the TV screen, upon which a brawny, bald-headed genie performed miraculous household chores, leaving everything spotless, while the words *an orphan* reverberated through his skull. All these years, he reflected, he had been an orphan without ever knowing it! Found in a basket on the doorstep, no less! Now they were sick of each other, and of him! With another, more penetrating chill through his lights and vitals, Jeff realized that he must leave this place he had mistakenly thought of as home for as long as he could remember, and that he must do so at once, before morning when his parents would, no doubt, return him to the authorities like a pet that has peed on the rug too many times and must finally be taken away.

Jeff quickly changed out of his pajamas, scrambled around his room grabbing an extra pair of socks and underpants, and his baseball mitt (which had taken two years to break in properly), and jammed all the stuff into his school briefcase. Then he took apart his coin bank, a plastic box molded to look like the US Treasury that he had acquired on a family (ha!) trip to the nation's capital. It contained over $30, mostly in quarters, and he stuffed a handful of the heavy coins in each of his pants pockets to more evenly distribute the weight. Finally, he put on his green loden duffle coat with the horn toggle buttons, took a last wistful look at the place that had been his room, and with tears blurring his vision tip-toed out of the apartment, the coins in his pockets jingling like sleigh bells.

He took the back stairs to avoid Leopold, the night doorman, and exited the apartment building via the service alley. Once outside on 79th Street, he realized that he had no destination whatever in mind. Then the episode of *The Twilight Zone* he had been watching came back to him, and the name Drakesburg in particular. He was old enough to know that TV shows happen in made-up places, but he thought that perhaps the fictional Drakesburg might be *based* on a real place of such a name, and he reasoned that it might be found by taking the train from Grand Central Station, just as the old man in the TV story had done.

A small, old-timey town like Drakesburg might be just the right place for an orphan to go and start life over again. In the city, no doubt, he would be tossed into some prison-like asylum for the misbegotten and unwanted, a hell-hole like the blacking factory in *Oliver Twist*. In a small town like Drakesburg, people were bound to be friendlier. In such a place, he might even be able to latch onto some *incomplete* family, like the one on the *Lassie* TV show—one with a mom, a grandpa, a kid, and a dog, but no father—and be happily welcomed into its midst, as long as he dutifully carried out his assigned chores. He didn't know how to milk a cow, but he was sure he could learn—farm boys did, and weren't many of them the offspring of *Republican morons,* as adults of his acquaintance referred to non-New Yorkers?

Consumed with these new ambitions, Jeff hailed a cab on the

corner of Madison and told the driver to take him to Grand Central Station, and not to try any funny stuff because he had made the trip a million times. The driver headed directly down Park Avenue, which, with its innumerable lighted Christmas trees, block after block, seemed all the more cheerless by sheer force of repetition. "Ever hear of a town named Drakesburg?" Jeff asked the driver as they passed the Soviet mission to the UN on Sixty-eighth Street, where Khrushchev had held forth from the balcony a few years earlier.

"Where?" the driver replied. "The Island? Jersey?"

"No, it's more New Englandy."

"Oh, the one where they had the big Civil War battle?"

"I don't know."

"Yeah, the Battle a'Drakesburg. It's famous. That's where they stemmed the tide."

"Do you know where that took place, by any chance?"

"Drakesburg. Where else?"

"I mean, what state?"

The driver hesitated as he pulled up to the train station on Vanderbilt Avenue. "You could try Massachusetts," he said. "It's historic and all."

"Thanks," Jeff said. He tipped the driver a quarter, as he had seen his parents do a thousand times (the memory made him shudder with emotion), and smashed through a ridge of slush to the entrance.

Grand Central was busy even at this late hour with holiday travelers coming and going for the weekend. Tomorrow, Saturday, would be Christmas Eve, making Sunday, of course, the Big Day. Inside the cavernous and seedy main waiting room, a five-piece Salvation Army band played carols at the foot of the grand stairway. In threadbare uniforms, they performed an especially lugubrious version of "We Three Kings" as Jeff hurried past to the brass-roofed information kiosk at the great room's center.

"I'm trying to get to a town called Drakesburg," he told a weary-looking man wearing a green eyeshade within the kiosk.

"What line?" the man replied to his 1,138th inquiry of the evening shift.

"I'm not sure. New England somewhere. Maybe Massachusetts."

"Got a Drakesville on the New Haven. It's in Vermont, just over your Massachusetts border."

"That must be it!" Jeff cried, electrified that his new life was taking shape so rapidly. Vermont, where there are more cows than people! He could practically hear them mooing to be milked! "When's the next train there?"

"The 11:20 Holiday Special to Montreal stops there."

"That's in ten minutes."

"Yup."

"Quick! Gimme a ticket!"

"I don't sell tickets. This is the information booth."

Jeff raced across the room to the wall of ticket windows and barked out his request.

"Round trip?" the agent inquired.

"One way," Jeff said, and a lump formed in his throat. "Hurry!"

"Sleeper or coach"

"What's the difference?"

"The sleeper, you get a berth."

"A birth . . . ?" Jeff reflected, preoccupied as he was with the mystery of his origins.

"A bed, like. To sleep on."

"Oh. Does it cost more?"

"You bet. Extra fifteen bucks."

"I'll just take the regular seat, please."

"Okay, that'll be seventeen-fifty." Jeff scooped two handfuls of quarters out of his pants pockets and pushed them under the grille.

"Whaja, rob a piggy bank, kid?"

The public address system announced final boarding for the Holiday Special to Montreal.

"Please hurry!"

"Hey, look, I gotta count this coin, you know," the agent said and then stopped what he was doing to stare for a moment at Jeff. "Say, what's a kid like you takin' a train for at this hour on a school night, anyway?"

"It's not a school night," Jeff said.

"Is that so?"

"Vacation already started."

"How come you're not with an adult?"

"None of your goddam business," Jeff said.

The agent recoiled behind his zoo-like window grill, but then, displaying a look of consternation, resumed counting the quarters and at last presented Jeff with a canary yellow ticket. "Some way to speak to your elders, sonny," he remarked. "Track nineteen."

Jeff raced across the slippery marble floor to the gate and hurried down the stairs. The platform level was poorly lighted, dirty, and smelled like something dredged out of the nether reaches of a refrigerator. Yet, he was thrilled at the sight of the idling train with its sleek silver cars and the crush of northbound travelers boarding with their shopping bags full of wrapped presents, who lent the otherwise grim underworld an oddly festive air.

"Sleeping cars up ahead!" a conductor bawled.

Jeff boarded a coach at the first open door and found a seat beside a window. The car filled up rapidly and soon Jeff heard a voice say, "Is this seat taken?"

"Nope."

An athletic, pug-faced young man chucked his suitcase in the rack overhead and slipped down into the aisle seat beside Jeff.

"You all alone?"

"Yup," Jeff said, and to him the answer was full of deep and tragic resonances. He wanted to tell the young man that he was, indeed, all alone, *all alone in the world,* that he was, in fact, an orphan, but he didn't want to seem pathetic, like the ragged, legless beggar lady who occupied a miserable square of sidewalk on a filthy blanket outside Bloomingdale's this time of year.

"Salty Parker." The young man offered his hand.

Jeff stared at it thinking that if he was an orphan, his name, Jeff Greenaway, was no longer valid, and that he ought not to use it anymore. He racked his brain for another.

"Chico Fernandez," he finally said, shaking hands. Chico Fernandez, of course, was the shortstop for the Detroit Tigers. It had just popped into his head. And now he was stuck with it.

"Chico Fernandez?" Salty said. "You any relation to the guy who plays shortstop for Detroit?"

"No." Jeff shook his head vigorously.

"I bet people ask you that all the time, huh?"

Jeff nodded.

"See, I go to school right outside of the Motor City," Salty said, adjusting his seat back and relaxing expansively. "University of Michigan, Ann Arbor. Just finished my last exam this morning. Been riding the G.D. train all the G.D. day since lunchtime."

"G.D.?"

Salty leaned in close. "Goddam," he whispered.

"Oh, well, Jeez, you must be good and goddam tired, then," Jeff said.

"I'm goddam bushed," Salty whispered. "I'da took a plane but my nerves can't take it. If the Lord meant for man to fly, he woulda given him propellers, right?"

Jeff cracked up at the remark until he remembered the tragic destiny that had led him to this particular seat next to Salty Parker on the 11:20 Holiday Special.

"Where you bound for, Chico?"

"Huh? Oh, Drakesville," Jeff said.

"Never heard of it."

"It's a beautiful New Englandy town way up north of here. They don't even have cars there yet."

Jeff realized at once that this was a preposterous statement, that he had confused TV with reality, but it was too late to retract it.

"How could they not have cars?" Salty said. "Cars are everywhere."

"Not in Drakesville. They don't allow 'em."

"How could they not allow 'em? This is America for criminy's sake!"

"They just don't, that's all. They don't want 'em cluttering up the town. They took a vote and that's how it came out."

"I never heard of anything like it."

7

"You ever been to Drakesville?"

"No."

"Believe me, it's much nicer without any cars."

"Well, how do people get around?"

"They walk."

"What if they have a big package? What if somebody's grandmother goes to the store and buys a refrigerator? I suppose she carries it home on her back."

"Of course not. For deliveries they have horses and wagons."

"You're kidding me."

"No, they do."

"Sounds like Disneyland–"

"All aboard!" the conductor shouted.

Moments later the train lurched forward. A pang of emotion, mostly fear, cut through Jeff as he realized the train was leaving the station, leaving New York City and everything that he knew. He fought an impulse to run down the aisle, leap out of the slow-moving car, and catch a taxi back home. But he was assailed by the fresh memory of his mother's mocking voice saying, ". . . a little orphan in a willow basket." He realized that no matter how odd and forlorn his present circumstances, he no longer had any home to go back to, and that the pathway of his future led, like the Holiday Special, to the mysterious north.

The train emerged from the dark underbelly of Park Avenue at 96th Street and picked up speed among the tenement gulches of Harlem. At this hour on a cold and slushy winter night, the streets were deserted. The train traversed the dreary Bronx in a matter of minutes and after that the world beyond the window became a dark blank. Only now did Jeff begin to consider all that he had left behind—besides two parents, who weren't even his to begin with, and a roomful of personal stuff. There were his classmates at Public School No. 6, including his best friend Bobby Skolnick. What would their teacher, Mrs. Snipes, say to the other kids? Perhaps nothing. Perhaps his parents—his *ex-parents*—would be too embarrassed to report his disappearance to the school authorities. But surely Bobby would call him at the apartment. All next week was Christmas vacation and they were supposed to go sledding on Pilgrim Hill in Central Park if there was snow, or go to the museum to visit the shrunken heads if there wasn't any snow. What would his mother—that is, the Greenaway woman—tell Bobby? He'd have to call Bobby when he got to Drakesville and explain the whole incredible situation. Maybe the Skolnicks could even adopt him. There was an empty bunk in Bobby's room, recently vacated by Bobby's older brother, Steve, who was sent away to boarding school. Jeff wouldn't mind sleeping on the living room couch when Steve came home for vacations—

"Tickets please!" the conductor cried.

"Hey, pal," Salty Parker addressed the conductor as he handed over his ticket to Holyoke, Massachusetts, "will you wake me up in time to get off in case I nod out?"

"Yessir."

"Me too," Jeff said. "By the way, what time does this train arrive at Drakesville?"

"Oh, 'bout six fifteen a.m."

"Jeez, I probably will conk out by then," Jeff said, sliding deep into his seat.

"Don't worry, son," the conductor said. "I'll wake you up in time. Your mama and pop gonna meet you there?"

"I don't have any parents," Jeff declared and Salty glanced at him with sudden curiosity. "I'm an orphan who was found on somebody's doorstep in a willow basket and they don't want me anymore."

The conductor, too, looked shocked for a moment, but then his cocoa-brown face melted into a warm smile and he said to Salty, "Ain't kids a riot? You two boys hit the hay if you want. I'll see to it that you wake up in time." And going *heh-heh-heh* in his bass voice, shaking his head at the foibles of children, the conductor lurched into the next car.

"Hey, are you really an orphan?" Salty asked, not so quick to laugh it off as the conductor had been.

"Yup."

"You live in an orphanage and all?"

"Not yet," Jeff said. "But I may have to apply to one soon."

"Well, where do you live?"

"New York, mostly."

"Who with?"

"These people," Jeff said, choking up a little.

"Like, foster parents?"

"No, they pretended to be real for a long time, but it turned out they were phonies."

"Gee, that's a rough break, Chico. Did you report 'em?"

"No. What's the point? I'd still be an orphan. And they'd still be phonies. I don't think it's against the law to be a phony, anyway."

"Sure it is. It's imposturing upon the morals of a minor."

"There just wasn't time—"

"You want me to report 'em for you?"

"No! I'll do it. I should be the one. Really."

"Okay. But make sure you do. They could imposture themselves on some other kid. Once they get a taste of it, you know, it goes on and on. They've gotta be stopped."

"Don't worry. I'll take care of it."

"You better, I'm telling you," Salty said, squirming out of his varsity jacket and pounding it into a kind of pillow. "Well, what are you gonna do now?"

"I'm moving up to this town, Drakesville."

"You got any relations there?"

"No. But they have these families you can move in with if you promise to milk the cows and take out the garbage. Usually there's no father because he got killed in the war, so they're glad to have an extra kid around."

"Gee, it sounds like TV," Salty said.

❋

10

Jeff was sound asleep when the conductor roused Salty Parker for the Holyoke stop. An hour later, the same conductor gently shook Jeff's shoulder as the train slowed in its approach to the Drakesville station. For a moment, panic seized him at waking up in such strange surroundings. He had no time to lose, however, for the train was grinding to a halt. And, while he had grave doubts about Drakesville living up to his expectations, he had no idea what lay up the tracks beyond it except, ultimately, Canada, a foreign country. Being an orphan was bad enough, he reasoned, but being both an orphan and a foreigner would be more than he could manage. So, he extracted himself from the cozy seat and, clutching the briefcase to his chest, prepared to get off the train.

It was still dark out, as dark as midnight, though the luminous hands of his Timex wristwatch read a quarter to six, practically morning. He was the only passenger who got off there and the train did not linger more than ten seconds after Jeff cleared the steps. Snow swirled in little tornadoes in the bleak electric light of the platform as the train picked up speed and vanished into the pre-dawn murk. Jeff had never felt cold like this. It made his nostrils feel stiff. Still clutching his briefcase, he revolved three hundred and sixty degrees to take in his new hometown. The station itself was closed at this hour, its small waiting room dark inside and without another living soul in evidence. Down a nearby street of ramshackle bungalows, a line of cars stood parked under rounded caps of fresh snow. So, there were cars after all, Jeff thought. He was disappointed but not so surprised. This was real life, not a TV show. Down another street in the opposite direction, a few streetlights burned fuzzily, illuminating buildings somewhat larger than the bungalows.

The street led past a grain depot and the dark hulk of a box mill to a bridge across a boisterous stream. Weird ice shapes like crystal knife blades had formed among the jumble of boulders that lined the streambed. Jeff leaned forward against the iron pipe railing and gazed down into the black torrent below. It occurred to him that wherever the stream came from, there would no doubt be waterfalls and pools and woods to explore in the summertime. There might be a lake up

11

there where the stream flowed out of the mountains. If milking cows for an incomplete family didn't work out, he thought, he could take off in the springtime and become a mountain hermit for a while. It also occurred to him that the bridge would be a good place to come and commit suicide if, God forbid, you were in the mood.

Across the bridge, stood a huge wood-framed building at least as big as Public School No. 6. Not a few of its windows emitted light and he could hear the hum and clank of machinery. A gold lettered sign over the entrance proclaimed it to be THE DRAKESVILLE DOW-EL WORKS. Not knowing what a dowel was he wondered if, perhaps, they had misspelled the word *towel*. The prospect of being the smartest person in the whole town rather thrilled him. He imagined himself going from one factory to another—also to shops and people's houses—correcting everybody's misspellings. He could probably even make some money at it, he thought, since people were constantly writing things down.

He moved on. Up a hilly street lined with darkened factory workers' houses, he encountered the town square. His heart soared—briefly. On closer inspection, the brick buildings surrounding the square looked run-down and dreary. The retail establishments there were not the old-timey soda fountains and penny-candy emporiums and cheerful general merchandise shops that he had imagined. On one side of the square was a drab auto parts store next to a pizzeria that featured slovenly signs in crude hand-lettering in the window, and which included more bad spelling. "Todays Special: Ital Potroast + mash or bake pot + salad/butt bread." Jeff was mystified about the meaning of *butt bread*. It sounded unappetizing, to say the least. The pizzeria's neighbor on the other side was a medical supply store with a window full of hernia trusses, bedpans, humidifiers, and artificial limbs. The proprietor had strewn ropes of winking Christmas lights among the prostheses, lending them more a creepy carnival air than a holiday feeling. The adjacent block featured two sleazy taverns, a beauty shop, and a realty office. One particular building on that side had been completely encased in turquoise aluminum paneling. Even the windows were paneled over. The heraldic insignia of a fraternal order was fastened to the center of the blank greenish-blue facade like monstrous tie tack.

As gray dawn light gathered over the rooftops, Jeff saw that the town square itself looked as bleak and empty as Siberia. Its elm trees had succumbed to the Dutch blight a decade earlier and had not been replaced. The bandshell he had expected to find there was conspicuously absent. The only object that occupied the square's snowy expanse was the statue of a Civil War soldier, cocked to one side on its pedestal by a century of frost heaves and looking rather like a drunk about to keel over.

As he had done at the station, Jeff rotated three hundred and sixty degrees taking in all the grim details of his newly chosen hometown. His toes and fingers ached from the cold. He remembered again that he was an orphan with no place to go, and standing at the edge of the desolate square he began to weep. Just then some lights flickered on in a shop front on the far side of the square, and then a neon sign that read "EAT" (spelled correctly, he was relieved to note).

It wasn't simply because he was the first customer of the day that Jeff attracted the combined stares of the grillman and both waitresses when he entered Lewis's Luncheonette. The truth was, none of them had ever seen an eleven-year-old boy in a long duffle coat carrying a leather briefcase, and all three adults regarded him as an ominous sight—some kind of midget on a sinister mission perhaps, or a process server, or a hired killer.

"Are you open?" Jeff inquired.

Reassured by the timbre of his voice that Jeff was only a child, the grillman said, "Ayuh," and resumed prepping his station.

Jeff shuffled up to the counter and took a seat on one of the revolving stools. On the rear counter, a cake-stand displayed a pyramid of blueberry muffins. Jeff fished around in his pocket to check his remaining funds. He made neat little stacks of coins on the counter and arrived at the figure $11.40.

"How much is hot cocoa and one of those muffins?" he asked.

"Cocoa's a dime and these here are fifteen cents," the plumper of the two waitresses said.

Jeff was thrilled. With $11.40, he calculated, he could live on muffins and hot chocolate for a week, if necessary. He ordered at once. The hot cocoa made him feel as though he were back in the land of the living, and he daintily picked apart the muffin, savoring every crumb. No meal in his recollection, however splendid—not even the chicken-a-la-king at Lindy's—had ever tasted so delicious. As he devoured the last morsels, one of the workers from the dowel factory came in for breakfast before the morning shift. He was a stout, middle-aged man in a red checked hunting shirt and plastic hat with three artificial fur flaps. Jeff tried to imagine how the front flap, the one over the eyes, was supposed to work.

"Merry Christmas, gals," the man said, dusting some snowflakes off his coat.

"'T'aint Christmas yet," the grillman said sourly over his shoulder.

"Well, it's Christmas Eve, ain't it?" the stout man said.

"'T'aint eve til evenin'."

"Aw, hell's bells—Christmas Eve *Day*, then, goddammit—"

"Luther!" the plump waitress said, nodding toward Jeff, to indicate that a child was present.

"Gonna be a white one, anyways," the other waitress chimed in from over at the coffee station.

"Always is," the grillman muttered.

This talk of Christmas and Christmas Eve depressed Jeff, for though he tried not to think about it, his mind turned to memories of Christmases past in the city that had been his home, and to the man and woman who had masqueraded as his parents all these years. Even though they were a couple of phonies, he couldn't help but think that, all in all, they had treated him decently and bought him a lot of presents over the years. Though claiming to be Jewish, they had always ignored the Hebrew holiday, Hanukkah, in favor of Christmas—obviously, he now realized, they hadn't been real Jews at all, only pretending. But then again, if *they* were not Jewish, then

14

what was *he?* Had there been a note left pinned to his willow basket informing the Greenaway couple what religious affiliation their orphan was?

"Lemme have two fried eggs and a short stack," Luther told the waitress.

"Meat?"

"Sausage, I guess."

The grillman flung three fat links on his griddle. They began to sizzle aromatically. Jeff noticed that he was still hungry, and for something more substantial than another muffin. Next, the grillman broke a couple of eggs in a pool of bubbling butter, and finally poured two dollops of pancake batter out beside the eggs.

"How much are sausages and flapcakes?" Jeff inquired.

"Eighty-five cents," the grillman said.

"Could you make me some?"

"Sure. You got eighty-five cents, little fella?"

"Oh, yeah. I'm loaded. Say, could you give me directions to the town orphanage, by any chance?"

"Orphanage? Don't know as we got one."

"Where do the orphans go, then?"

"Beats me. Don't know as we got any of them, neither. Why? Are you an orphan?"

"As a matter of fact, yes. I became one rather recently."

"Poor thing," Jeff's waitress said. "What happened to your folks?"

"Nothing."

"Nothing? You mean they didn't die in a car wreck or nothing?"

"No. They were impostors."

"Impostors? I never heard of any such thing."

"It's an unusual case," Jeff said.

"But why would anybody do that?"

"To get married," Jeff said.

"Wait a minute," the waitress said. "They pretended to be your parents so they could get married?"

"Yup."

"Usually it's the other way around."

15

Jeff realized he could never explain it.

Just then, the grillman barked to the waitress to pick up Jeff's order of flapcakes and sausages. As he addressed his plate, the establishment began to fill up with other men on their way to work, and the waitresses scurried around, taking orders. When he was finished, he left a twenty-five-cent tip, since he was planning to be around Drakesville for a while, and might take more meals in the luncheonette.

Outside, full daylight had erased the gloom of dawn. Only a few random flakes floated down in the breezeless air. Cars now glided around the square and more lights flickered on in the other shop fronts. A few people plied the sidewalks. Signs of life eased the town's initially stark, forbidding look.

Briefcase in hand, Jeff set forth to explore his new home. On the side of town farthest from the train station and the dowel factory lay streets with some very imposing old houses. Many had porches and some had delightful towers, turrets, bays, oriels, and cupolas. Jeff wondered about the families who lived inside, and how he might go about applying for adoption. With no orphanage in town, he reasoned, he would have to make all the arrangements himself and, with no prior experience, he was puzzled about the procedure. For instance, should he just go up, ring a doorbell, and ask to be shown around? He preferred to have a room of his own. Having no siblings all his life, he wondered about the relative advantages of choosing a family with children younger or older than himself, and whether they should be boys or girls. He didn't think it would be a good idea to move in with a childless couple who lacked parenting experience. They might get sick of him the way the Greenaways had.

Jeff was encouraged by his stroll around the neighborhood, though he didn't ring any doorbells just yet. He even passed a group of other children pulling sleds behind them, and they seemed to be very *normal* American types, like the kids on TV. Back in the city, a snowfall was a special occasion. Here in Drakesville, evidently, you could go sledding every day. Shortly, he passed the town grammar school, a quaint old sandstone building with a mansard roof, and a clock tower, and a yard with a real baseball backstop and wooden dugouts. The yard at Public School No. 6 had been a wasteland of asphalt pavement enclosed by a cyclone fence that made it look like the setting of *Riot in Cellblock D.*

Circling back toward the town square, on a street magically called Elm, he encountered the Strand Theater, an art deco relic with an odd triangular marquee. The sight of it struck Jeff with a special urgency because the movie showing that week was *West Side Story.* He didn't know what the movie was about, exactly, but he had a strong hunch that it took place in his ex-hometown, New York. A throng of children, plus a few teenagers, and even parents, waited in line under the marquee to buy tickets for the noon matinee. Jeff was cold and rather hungry again after his long walk around town. But he didn't see the point of returning to the luncheonette for a hamburger when he could fill up on popcorn and candy, see a movie, and stay warm for several hours, all for little more than the price of a hot meal.

Besides, he felt a certain proprietary compulsion to monitor the reactions of these country folk while they watched a movie about a place he undoubtedly knew better than any of them. So, he lined up with his new fellow townspeople and bought a ticket. It was fifty cents. Inside, he purchased a medium buttered popcorn, a roll of Necco wafers, a Charleston Chew bar, and a large orange soda, all for another $1.50, leaving him with $7.80 for the rest of his childhood in Drakesville. But he made up his mind that when the movie was over, he would return to the neighborhood of nice older houses and present himself for adoption. How could they turn down an orphan on Christmas Eve, he thought?

The movie opened with a swooping panoramic helicopter view of Manhattan Island. The shot made Jeff recall his favorite haunts around the enchanted isle: the armor gallery in the Metropolitan Museum of Art, the shrunken-head room at the Museum of Natural History, the gorilla house at the Central Park Zoo, the Horn and Hardart Automat on Fifty-seventh Street, the first-floor game showroom of Abercrombie & Fitch. The memories left him feeling so homesick that he nearly lost his appetite. But then the action started with the Puerto Rican and white gangs having a "rumble," as gang fights were called

17

then, and the characters stopping what they were doing to sing a song every eleven minutes.

And even though he grew monumentally bored with the romance between "Tony" and "Maria," Jeff was able to forget about his plight for a while. When the movie ended, he decided to stick around and see the beginning over again, largely because he dreaded the task that awaited him outside. But the movie, with its romantic goo and inane caterwauling, was so unwatchable a second time that he got up and left before the Jets gang finished boasting in song about their many accomplishments and distinctions.

When he left the theater, it was snowing again. Two inches of fresh powder carpeted the sidewalks, and he wished that he had thought to bring his galoshes. Nevertheless, he set forth once again for the neighborhood of nice older homes, briefcase still in hand. It was that hour of a winter afternoon, still long before supper time, when the days are shortest and twilight gathers softly in the eaves and the air takes on a purplish hue. Many of Drakesville's houses wore Christmas decorations, but they tended toward the sedate and conservative. There were no blinking electric reindeer scaling rooftops, no life-sized plastic Santas on the lawns, just dark swags of fir and beribboned wreaths and here and there a few twinkling lights on the porches. A block past the fabulous school building, he paused before a large white colonial house—built when America really was a colony—and decided to make his first inquiry there.

The woman who answered the doorbell was as big and broadhipped as a Holstein cow, and she wore cats-eye eyeglasses that were too small for her head. Her smile was as outsized as the rest of her, however, and she greeted Jeff warmly.

"Why, hello young man."

"I, uh, uh, uh. . . ."

"Won't you come in?"

He was happy to step in from the cold. The house was nicely furnished with old things, and a lighted balsam pine tree, surrounded by a heap of presents, seemed to occupy an inordinate amount of space in the adjacent living room. Jeff surmised that the family was well-off and might be able to take him in. He wasn't thrilled by the idea of having such an unglamorous new mother—no doubt his new friends would make cracks about her—but she seemed kindly, and he could always explain that they weren't actually related.

"You must be the twins' new friend from school."

"I, uh—*huh?*"

"I'll call them. Oh, Tammy, Chrissie!" she hollered melodically to the house's dim interior, from which a luscious smell of baking cookies wafted. Almost at once two girls Jeff's age came thundering down the hall. They were identical twins, each a small replica of the mother. They wore matching jumpers that intensified the eerie effect of duplication. Both had on eyeglasses too small for their heads. One of them—Tammy? Chrissie?—had chocolate smeared around her cheeks and double chin. The girls eyed Jeff with suspicion.

"He's no friend of ours," they both said absolutely in unison.

"I, uh, must have the wrong house," Jeff mumbled, retreating toward the door.

"Well, I never. . . ." he heard the woman say as he stumbled back out into the snowy twilight. Though this family had proven unsuitable, Jeff was not discouraged. To the contrary, he was quite pleased with himself for having gone through with it, and he realized that success on the first try was unrealistic, anyway. So, spirits bolstered, he ventured deeper into the neighborhood.

Around the corner on Walnut Street stood a fine red brick dwelling with handsome green shutters. Jeff had no doubt that the family in residence was financially secure, and he was thrilled to discover a brass plate above the doorbell with the name "Drake" engraved on it in fancy script. Possibly this was the very family that the town was named after. He rang the bell, brimming with confidence.

A college-aged man answered the doorbell. He was rail-thin and attired in a rather peculiar costume: pajamas and a green plaid bathrobe, with a crew-neck sweater over the top part of the robe. A cigarette with an extraordinarily long ash at its tip dangled from the corner of his mouth. He had not shaved for several days. His red- rimmed eyes blinked continually, and an acrid smell wafted off him.

"Yes?" he said.

"Hello, I'm an orphan," Jeff declared, having decided to come right to the point, "and I was wondering if you or your family have ever thought of adopting one."

The man removed the cigarette from his mouth in order, it seemed, to gape more dramatically at Jeff. "You're kidding me?" he said, and then emitted a brief, quasi-giggle that signified something besides simple amusement.

"No, it's the truth," Jeff assured him. "Is your mom or dad home, by any chance?"

"Mom's been dead a year now," young Drake said, issuing another abbreviated giggle before practically jamming the cigarette back into his face. When he exhaled, an unnatural quantity of smoke boiled out of his nostrils. Just then, heavy footsteps resounded beyond the entrance foyer. An older man soon appeared, sixty or so, but large and hale, wearing a necktie with a cardigan sweater.

"Who said you could leave your room, Walter?" he asked angrily.

"Look, Pop," Walter said. "A little Christmas elf dropped by to visit."

"Go on, get back upstairs."

Walter didn't resist the command, but before departing, he smiled concupiscently at Jeff and, expelling another sinister cloud of smoke, said, "Goodbye little elf."

The older man watched Walter disappear completely upstairs before turning back to Jeff and saying, "What do you want?"

"Nothing," Jeff said.

"Then go away and don't come back," the man said and closed the heavy front door an inch from Jeff's nose.

Jeff was more bewildered than discouraged by the encounter. He had wanted to explain that he was an orphan, not an elf, but something told him that the head of this household wouldn't care one way or the other. In any case, he made a mental note to cross this particular family off his list.

At the next house he tried, nobody was home, though a tree festooned with multicolored lights glowed within. The house after that was a gloom-cloaked colossus in the ponderous Queen Anne style. He could not locate a doorbell, only a heavy brass knocker cast into a visage that looked vaguely like something Lon Chaney once had played in a movie. The resounding *thunk* it produced summoned to the door a bony, blue-haired lady who appeared annoyed at having been disturbed. When Jeff explained that he was an orphan, et cetera, she looked him up and down as though he were some figure of odium and contempt, a tramp, say, and in a voice full of broken reeds told him, "I've more than half a mind to call the constable, sonny boy."

"No, don't—" Jeff tried to plead with her, though he had already eliminated her as a candidate.

"Orphan, indeed! Why I never. . . ." she muttered, closing the oaken door so hard that the leaded panes rattled in the sidelights.

Jeff hurried back down to the sidewalk, afraid that the police would soon arrest him for every unsolved crime perpetrated in Drakesville since the days of Franklin D. Roosevelt. By now, night had stolen over the town. Jeff's hands were so numb that he had to constantly switch carrying his briefcase from his right hand to his left hand and back again while he tried unsuccessfully to warm them by turns in his coat pocket. How, he wondered, could anyone fail to understand his situation? Where was the America that he had heard about at Public School No. 6? The people who had freed the slaves and beat the Nazis? As he pondered these elusive mysteries of modern culture, he wended his way through the darkening streets, unable to summon the will to ring another doorbell. His path eventually led back toward the town square. The luncheonette's neon sign flickered fuzzily up ahead through the falling snow. Jeff hurried over to it and dashed inside.

"Can I get a hamburger?" Jeff asked, shivering on a stool at the counter.

"We're closed," the grillman said, scraping down his griddle.

"It's *him* again," Jeff heard the chubby waitress whisper to the thinner one as they sat at a table sorting the day's checks. A lush orchestral arrangement of Christmas carols gushed out of a radio above the coffee station. All satin and silver filigree styling, the songs reminded him again of Christmas in New York, of the happy crowds on Madison Avenue laden with shopping bags, and the wonderful store window displays with big tin soldiers that moved. And of the skaters crowding the rink at Rockefeller Center under the gilded statue of Prometheus, and of the immense tree at the Metropolitan Museum of Art, with half the population of ancient Judea represented in clay figures at its base, and suddenly he couldn't stand the rush of memories anymore and burst out bawling on his revolving stool. Nothing would avail to stop him, not the waitresses' attempts to calm him down, nor the grillman's pleas that it was nearly five o'clock on Christmas Eve "for Gawdsake" and they had to close the place. Jeff was so carried away by his grief that he didn't notice the skinny waitress go to the pay phone and call the authorities.

Chief of Police Calvin Burdock—of a force of four, including the secretary—drove up in a matter of minutes. The tall, somewhat stooped Chief Burdock, with his kindly concave face, wearing a gray wool hunting coat over his khaki uniform, took a seat on the stool beside Jeff's, put his big hand on the boy's shoulder and, in a voice full of the calm of northern forests on a snowy night, asked Jeff his name more than several times until, at least, the boy stopped bawling and blew his nose with a napkin provided by the chubby waitress.

"What's your name, son?" Burdock asked for the ninth time with no evident loss of patience.

"Chico Fernandez," Jeff said.

"I hear you're an orphan, Chico," Burdock said.

Jeff nodded his head.

"Where's your home?"

"Orphans don't have homes," Jeff said. "If they had homes, they wouldn't *be* orphans."

"Of course," Burdock agreed. "But you must come from somewhere."

"I was found on a doorstep in a willow basket," Jeff said, and started to cry again, though not as violently as before.

22

"Chief," the grillman said, "I've got to drive over to to Bellow's Falls tonight, and with this storm and all...."

Chief Burdock said he understood. Normally in such a case where no law had been broken, the police might bring an apparent runaway child like Jeff to the hospital in Brattleboro for safekeeping and observation while the parents were located. But since it was Christmas Eve, with a snowstorm imminent, and since the chief had commitments of his own, he decided the best thing to do was to bring the boy home with him.

"Come with me, Chico," he said.

"Please don't put me in jail."

"You're not going to jail."

"Where are you gonna take me, then?"

"Well. . . home," Burdock said, and the word had an effect on Jeff like the electric current that lighted all the Christmas trees on Park Avenue.

Chief Burdock allowed Jeff to sit in the front seat of the police cruiser as they swung around the square and headed down Walnut Street.

"There's a weird guy in that house who walks around in his pajamas all day," Jeff remarked as they passed the Drake establishment. The chief merely coughed in reply, having at his disposal a good deal of privileged information about the Drake family's calamities.

Eventually, Walnut Street turned into a twisting country road. The snowflakes rushed at them in the car's headlight beams like anti-aircraft flak. The countryside lay hidden in the darkness.

"Where you from, Chico?" Chief Burdock asked.

"I told you. I was left on a doorstep in a willow basket."

"Well, yes. But where was the doorstep?"

Jeff hesitated a moment, and then said, "Iowa," because he had been assigned to do a report on Iowa in school, and he knew about its products (corn, pork), and the state flower (wild rose), in case he

23

was pressed for details. But all Chief Burdock said was, "That's a fair piece from here."

Fuzzy lights in the distance soon resolved themselves into the forms of a white farmhouse and a red barn in a little hollow that could have come straight off a greeting card. Jeff's heart leaped as Chief Burdock turned in the driveway.

"Is this where you live?"

"Ayuh."

"Is your family complete?"

"Beg your pardon. . . ?"

"Any members missing? Your wife or kids?"

"Not that I know of," Chief Burdock said as they pulled up to the side porch and a woman appeared behind a storm door. She looked young and attractive in a wholesome way. In fact, Jeff was staring at her so intently that he failed to notice that Chief Burdock had cut the engine and thrown the door open. "Come on, Chico," the chief said and Jeff followed him inside.

It was an old-fashioned kitchen with a great wooden table upon which were deployed the implements of pie-making and several specimens of pie. A fireplace blazed along the far wall. Delicious cooking aromas penetrated every receptive quarter of Jeff's skull as he took it all in. Something succulent was roasting away in the oven—a haunch of deer or moose, he wondered? Jeff was in such a rapture that he failed to see another boy his age quietly enter the room. The boy bore a striking resemblance to Chief Burdock, his face also somewhat dish-shaped, but he was an inch or two taller than Jeff.

"Chico. . . ?"

"Huh—?"

"I'd like you to meet Mrs. Burdock—Mary—and my son, Chester," the Chief said.

"Chester?" Jeff repeated, thrilled. "Like Marshall Dillon's sidekick on TV?"

The other boy nodded his head sheepishly as though he'd heard this many times before, but he stuck his hand out to shake.

"Everyone calls me Chet," he said.

"Say Chet," the chief said. "Why don't you take Chico here out to the barn and show him Sarge?"

"Sure, Pop."

"Who's this Sarge?" Jeff inquired, thinking it sounded like an officer in whose ill-tempered custody he would now be placed.

"Sarge is my horse," Chet said.

"You've got a horse? God. . . !"

"Sure. Come on. I'll show him to you."

"What'd you say your name was?" Chet asked as they entered the barn.

"Chico Fernandez," Jeff replied, gazing at the huge, dim interior in wonder. He had never been in a real barn before. The loft was filled with bales of hay, which scented the air with an odd but lovely summery aroma. Old tools and harness hung from the massive posts and beams.

"Say, are you any relation to the fella who plays third base for the Dee-troit Tigers?" Chet asked.

"Not that I know of."

"I saw that show, *The West Side Story*, up to the Strand, and you don't look Spanish."

"I'm not. It's a nickname, actually."

"I never heard of any nickname that had a last name."

"We had a guy in our bunk at camp that everyone called Mighty Mouse."

"Anyways, what's your reg'lar name?"

"I'm not sure. I'm an orphan."

"Oh. . . ." Chet let it drop and entered a box stall. "This here's Sarge," he said proudly, bringing forward a big sorrel horse, whose nostrils discharged great huffing clouds of steam. Chet stroked the animal's cheek and fed him a carrot. "Go ahead, you can touch him."

Jeff hesitated, then reached up and petted Sarge's nose. "It's all velvety!" he cried.

"We have a lot of fun, Sarge and me. Only he's real stubborn. You always have to let him know who's boss."

"Can you ride him whenever you want?"

"Sure. 'Cept during school hours."

"God. . . . How old are you?"

"Eleven."

"Jeez, me too. When's your birthday?"

"June thirteenth."

"You're kidding!"

"Nope."

"Mine's June twelfth! Isn't that an amazing coincidence?"

"I guess it is."

"Could we ride Sarge tomorrow maybe?"

"Sure. I guess. After the Christmas stuff."

"What Christmas stuff?" Jeff asked, imagining for a moment some rite of prayer and supplication he was unacquainted with.

"The presents and all like that."

"Oh," Jeff said, lowering his gaze to the hay-strewn floor.

Observing Jeff's sudden plunge into melancholy, Chet ventured to broach the delicate subject. "Chico, where are you from?" he asked.

"Oh, I've been all over: Iowa, New York, Transylvania. When you're an orphan, you have to move around a lot."

"What happened to you?"

"I got booted out. My so-called parents turned out to be a couple of phonies."

"Gosh!"

"Yeah, it was a big disappointment. Boy, was I ever surprised."

"I'll bet."

"Hey, Chet, would you be upset if I asked your parents to adopt me?"

Chet flinched—the idea was so startling.

"Naw," he eventually said. "Go ahead and ask 'em."

"Hey, that's really great. Only, don't say I mentioned it, okay? I don't want to seem pushy."

"All right."

"It's just that, you know, when you're a kid, you need a place to take a bath and all."

"Sure."

"Not that I'm dirty."

They returned to the warm house to find a sumptuous feast laid across the great table. Chief Burdock carved a baked ham studded with cloves and garnished with pineapple rings. "Mmm-mmm," Chet said, rubbing his hands together.

"What kind of meat is that?" Jeff inquired.

"Why, it's a ham, Chico," Mary Burdock said. "What else did you suppose it might be?"

"Moose?"

"Pshaw!"

"Guess what, Pop," Chet said. "Chico's birthday is the day right before mine, June twelfth."

"How do you like that?" Mary Burdock said.

"And he's from all over—New York, Pennsylvania—"

"How much does it cost to get a horse?" Jeff interrupted so as to quash the subject of his origins.

"Depends on the animal," Chief Burdock said.

"One like Sarge."

"Oh, well, Chet raised him up from a colt for a 4-H project."

"Could I do that? Raise up a horse of my own from a baby?"

"I don't see why not," Mary Burdock said.

The chief cut a glance at his wife. "Okay, everyone. Have a seat. Pass up your plate, son."

Supper itself took a soberer turn. Jeff worried that he had insinuated himself a little too brashly, talking about the horse as though he were scheming to stick around for a while. But the truth was that the Burdock family had entered a kind of feeding transport, concentrating fiercely on the contents of their plates. This was rather different table behavior than Jeff was accustomed to back in New York, where the Greenaway woman and her husband had blabbed their way through entire meals, sometimes both talking at the same time. Unbeknownst to Jeff was the additional fact that while he had been out in the barn with Chet, Chief Burdock had put in a call to the state police in Brattleboro, who had an all-points bulletin out of New York City on an eleven-year-old boy who fit Jeff's description exactly. And the state police, in turn, had notified the anguished parents about Chief Burdock's discovery in faraway Drakesville.

After a luscious desert of apple crumb pie with ice cream, there was a rush among the family to get into town for the Christmas Eve service, what with the roads so sloppy, and drifts beginning to accumulate where the woods gave onto open fields. But, at eight o'clock sharp, Jeff found himself in a wooden pew near the front of the two-hundred-year-old Congregational church surrounded by an excited, buzzing crowd of red-cheeked Vermonters. He had never attended an actual church service—though he had peeked inside the entrance of St. Patrick's Cathedral once or twice, with its exotic odor of incense and spooky medieval interior. He'd never been in a synagogue, either, since the Greenaways were non-practicing, and none of his friends had yet attained the age of the bar mitzvah. But the cheerful, heady scene in the Drakesville Congregational church, with its fir swags draped along the balcony, and the austere lines of its architecture, and an organ playing familiar carols, appealed to him very much. The people seemed like the kind of folk he had seen only in Jimmy Stewart movies. The service proper was festive, short on prayer, and long on caroling. A twenty-member choir led the congregation in all the favorites, most of which Jeff knew the tunes to, if not the lyrics. The minister, a jolly man who oddly resembled Mr. Peevis, the principal of Public School No. 6, gave a seven-minute sermon about peace on earth and loving thy neighbor, and then, as the organ launched into a muscular version of "Joy to the World," the congregation was dismissed. Dozens of townspeople buttonholed Chief Burdock as he made his way up the aisle, and Jeff glowed with the prospect of joining one of the most beloved families in all of Drakesville.

28

Outside, it had stopped snowing, and the trip home—that is, to the Burdock farm—was a Currier and Ives lithograph of Christmas in New England come-to-life, with the moon emerging over a distant mountaintop, the snow sparkling as though it were composed of silver glitter, the tree boughs hung with white sleeves drooping low along the road, and, over it all, a wonderful rural stillness that seemed to hold back time so that Christmas and childhood might last forever.

Mrs. Burdock set up a cot for Jeff in Chet's room. It was discovered that Jeff's briefcase contained only one pair of clean socks and underpants (and a Jimmy Piersall model fielder's glove), so he borrowed a pair of pajamas from Chet. The chief came in for a minute to wish them good night and to warn them against opening presents before he and Mrs. Burdock got up. Then he turned off the light and closed the door. But moonlight flooded through the window, and as new friends who take a liking to each other will, the boys stayed awake for hours, Jeff bragging of his adventures in New York City and Transylvania, and Chet telling yet more astounding tales of the eight-point buck he had shot with his father that fall, and of lunker trout that lurked in certain pools of Black Brook, and of the first time he rode Sarge clear over to Newfane to impress his twelve-year-old cousin, Jenny, who was the most beautiful girl in all of Windham County (if you cared about that sort of thing), until all their tales became a dream of flying horses and Jeff fell sound asleep.

The warning about opening presents too early proved unnecessary because the boys didn't wake up until Mary Burdock put the bacon on to fry. Then, after a big waffle breakfast, everybody went into the parlor, as it was called, to open presents. Mary Burdock went first, wrestling with an enormous box that revealed one those new electric toaster-ovens that was making the tedium of cookery a thing of the past for modern women. Then Chet opened his first present: a fly-tying kit. Next, Mary Burdock handed Jeff a box, saying, "Merry Christmas, Chico, dear." He was amazed. He'd assumed that there hadn't been time for anyone to get presents for him, or even discover what kinds of things he liked, so he had not expected anything. In any case, he thanked the Burdocks lavishly and then ripped the wrapping paper off the box, which turned out to contain a jigsaw puzzle of a duck-hunting scene.

The truth was, Jeff loathed puzzles, especially of the jigsaw variety. But he was so grateful to receive anything, and took it as such a promising sign of his prospects, that he gushed over it at length, admiring the artistry of the duck-hunting scene ("They're pintails!" Chet informed him), and exclaiming on the degree of difficulty it called for ("It'll probably take a million years to finish!" he said), so that the effort nearly exhausted him.

The chief got a green-checked wool hunting shirt from Chet. Mrs. Burdock got a blender (more household tedium vanquished), and Chet got a camping knife with a fork and spoon that cleverly folded onto its sides, and a leather pouch to wear on his belt. Jeff was given a floppy package that proved to be a pair of pajamas. If you included the pair he had borrowed from Chet, he figured he now had enough pajamas to last through junior high school. One thing he wouldn't have to worry about any more was pajamas, he remarked, thank God for that, and everybody agreed. Finally, with a pretty good imitation of fanfare—Mary Burdock singing *tum-tah-tah-tum*—the chief brought forth a long, skinny package that had been hidden behind the rear of the tree, and handed it to Chet.

"Aw, Pop," Chet said. With eyes glistening, he tore into the red metallic wrapping. Shortly, a Remington bolt-action varmint rifle emerged.

"Gosh, it's a beaut!"

"Jeez," Jeff exclaimed in admiration (and envy), "a BB gun!"

"It's not a BB gun. It's a twenty-two."

"A real rifle?" Jeff gasped.

"That's right, Chico," the chief said.

To Jeff, this was a Christmas present beyond anybody's wildest imaginings—surely beyond anything plausible in the world he came from. In New York City, a parent would no more give his eleven-year-old child a rifle than he would give it a Diner's Club card. To live in a place where a boy could have a rifle of his very own, and a real horse to go with it, was so outlandishly fantastic that Jeff wondered for a moment why he hadn't run away sooner.

"Can we take it out and try her, Pop?" Chet asked.

"I don't see why not. Go get dressed, boys."

They hurried upstairs, where Chet lent Jeff a flannel shirt and a pair of *dungarees* as Vermonters called blue jeans. When they got out back behind the house, Chief Burdock had just finished tying a big tomato juice can to a string from the limb of an apple tree. He produced a box of bullets from deep in his pants pocket and handed them to Chet.

"Lock and load, son."

Chet slipped a cartridge into the chamber and closed the bolt.

"Fire at will, son."

The can spun wildly on its string while the report of the gunshot echoed off the distant hillside a full second later. The spicy smell of cordite hung in the still cold air.

"She shoots great, Pop!"

"We'll have to sight her in on a bench rest, of course."

Chet took several more shots, hitting the can every time, and then casually handed the rifle to Jeff. "You try a few, Chico."

"Me?"

"Sure."

"God. . . !"

The rifle was really heavy, Jeff observed. More than two baseball bats.

"Your safety's that little red button there on the trigger-guard, son," Chief Burdock said, handing over some bullets. "Lock and load, Chico."

Jeff eased a bullet into the breach just as he'd watched Chet do. The mechanical precision of the bolt thrilled him. The tomato juice can looked as tiny as a flyspeck in his sights fifty feet away. He closed his eyes just before he pulled the trigger and missed the target.

Just then, Mary Burdock came out the back door in her shirtsleeves and called to her husband. "Cal, would you come here for a minute?"

"Ayuh," he replied. "You boys be careful, now."

While the chief was inside, Chet offered Jeff a little shooting instruction—how to hold the weapon, how to squeeze the trigger instead of jerking it, and to keep his eyes open when he fired. By the time Chief Burdock reemerged from the house, Jeff had hit the can several times.

"Uh, Chico, would you come inside for a minute, please?"

"Sure," Jeff said, handing the rifle back to Chet. He figured now that Christmas was officially over, he'd have to start doing some chores to earn his keep. Still, to live in a place like this with an adopted brother like Chet, and with a horse and a real rifle, was worth doing a few chores. He hadn't noticed any cows in the barn, so he supposed that they wanted him to take a pail of water out for Sarge. Imagine his shock when he stepped into the parlor and found the Greenaways sitting together on the sofa.

"Jeff!" his mother cried and flew across the room, engulfing him in her arms. His father followed in a more measured male manner.

"Get away from me!" Jeff screamed and wriggled away.

"Jeff, please!" his mother sobbed.

"Impostors! Fakes! Phonies!" he shouted at them. "They're not my parents."

His mother took a couple of steps toward him, but Jeff kept backing away.

"Please, pussycat," his mother continued to sob. "What is it? What's the matter? Why did you run away?"

"You know why. 'Cause I'm an orphan. You only got married 'cause someone stuck me on your doorstep in a willow basket. I hate you."

"Son. . . ." his father advanced a step.

"Keep away!" Jeff said. "Help! Help! Chet, help!"

Chief Burdock, unsure what to do, seized Jeff by the shoulders. "Calm down, son," he said.

"Leggo of me!" Jeff howled.

Suddenly Chet rushed into the room, the rifle in his hands.

"Plug 'em, Chet! Quick! Save me!"

"I can't shoot people, Chico."

"Put the rifle away, son," Chief Burdock said.

By this time, sensing it was hopeless, Jeff collapsed in a blubbering heap at Chief Burdock's feet. It was quickly arranged for the Greenaways to go upstairs with Jeff to the Burdocks' bedroom, to try to reason with him. And though it took almost two hours, they eventually succeeded in persuading him that he was not an orphan, that he was their son, that they had legal documents to prove it, that what he had overheard on Friday night was all a terrible misunderstanding, and that they were very, very sorry.

All in all, Jeff was relieved to have his familiar world reconstructed and returned to him, and as the now reconciled Greenaway family prepared to depart in their rented car, he was even able to recall a few cherished details about the city that was his home—the shrunken head gallery at the Museum of Natural History, Yankee Stadium, the faces of his friends back at Public School Number 6, the first floor game showroom of Abercrombie and Fitch, and so on. But it was with a palpable sense of reluctance and regret that he departed the Burdock farm that Christmas afternoon.

For some months after that, he exchanged letters with Chet— who continued to call him *Chico*—and there was some fairly serious talk among the Greenaways and the Burdocks about letting Jeff come up to visit in June, when the boys could ride Sarge and shoot varmints and catch lunker trout in Black Brook. But the truth was that Jeff knew if he returned to Drakesville he might never want to come back to the city again. So, he made various excuses until summer commenced, and the whole Greenaway family went off to their rented cottage on Nantucket, where the whalefishes blow.

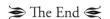

The End

Made in the USA
Lexington, KY
15 November 2019

56975793R00027